Shoes

"One, two, three, four, five, once I caught a fish alive..." sang Fimbo. He was fishing in the Playdips.

"Glung! Bet you can't catch me!" giggled Rockit.

"Of course not! You're a frog, not a fish!" laughed Fimbo, as his nose started to twitch. "Oh! I'm getting the Fimbling Feeling! Perhaps I'll catch a fish."

Fimbo lifted up the rod and found... a shoe on the end.

"It's not a fish, it's a shoe!" he said. "I wish it was a fish! Perhaps I'll go and show Pom the shoe, and come back later to see if I've caught anything."

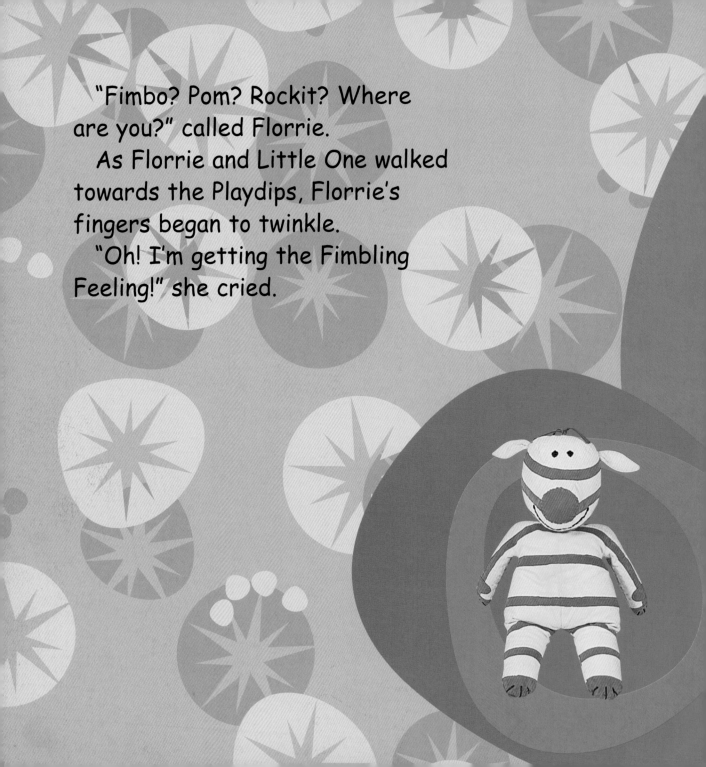

"Fimbo? Pom? Rockit? Where are you?" called Florrie.

As Florrie and Little One walked towards the Playdips, Florrie's fingers began to twinkle.

"Oh! I'm getting the Fimbling Feeling!" she cried.

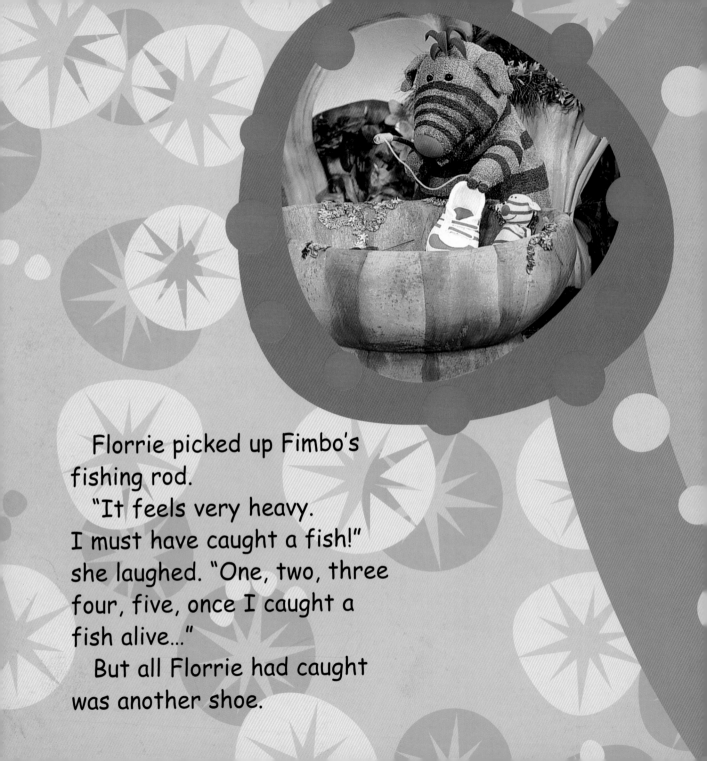

Florrie picked up Fimbo's fishing rod.

"It feels very heavy. I must have caught a fish!" she laughed. "One, two, three four, five, once I caught a fish alive..."

But all Florrie had caught was another shoe.

Fimbo came back with Baby Pom,
to see if he had caught a fish yet.
"Look!" he said. "I found a shoe, too."
"Fimbo, your shoe is the same as
mine!" cried Florrie.

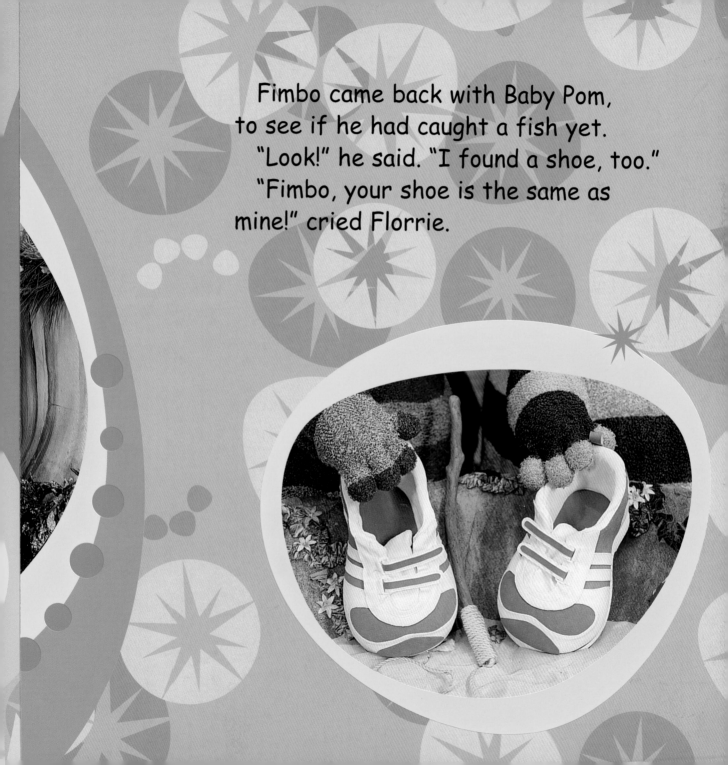

"Fimbo really wants to catch a fish," said Florrie to Baby Pom, at the Busy Base. "I know! Let's make a fish for Fimbo!"

Florrie got a piece of paper from the Busy Box, put the shoe on top, and drew around it with a pencil.

Then she cut the shape out. It looked like a fish.

"Shoe fish!" shouted Baby Pom. She and Florrie stuck an eye, scales and a tail onto the shoe fish.

"Maybe I should wish for a fish," Fimbo
was saying to Rockit at the Playdips.

"Wissshhhh for a fissshhhh," chanted
Rockit, waving his arms.

Fimbo was so busy watching Rockit, he
didn't see Florrie slipping the shoe fish
into the Playdips.

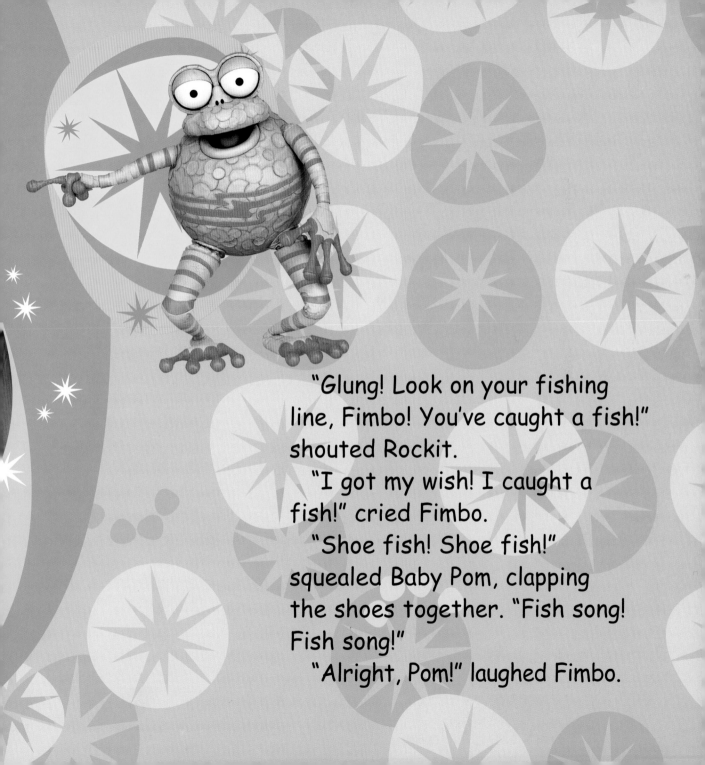

"Glung! Look on your fishing
line, Fimbo! You've caught a fish!"
shouted Rockit.

"I got my wish! I caught a
fish!" cried Fimbo.

"Shoe fish! Shoe fish!"
squealed Baby Pom, clapping
the shoes together. "Fish song!
Fish song!"

"Alright, Pom!" laughed Fimbo.

"One, two, three, four, five,
Once I caught a fish alive.
Six, seven, eight, nine, ten,
Then I let it go again.
Why did you let it go?
Because it bit my finger so!
Which finger did it bite?
This little finger on my right!"

1
2
3
4
5
6 7 8 9 10